THE GREAT BOOK OF LEGENDARY
WITCHES & WIZARDS

whitestar·kids

CONTENTS

INTRODUCTION 4
MORGAN LE FAY 6
The Legend of Morgan and King Arthur - *England* 8
MERLIN AND VIVIAN 12
The Legend of the Brocéliande Forest - *France* 16
CIRCE 18
The Legend of Circe and Odysseus - *Greece* 20
MELINDA 24
The Legend of Melinda - *Italy* 26
TÁLTOS 30
The Legend of the Seventh Year - *Hungary* 32
THE WITCH OF GIRONA 34
The Legend of the Cathedral of Girona - *Spain* 36
UNDINES 38
The Legend of Lorelei - *Germany* 40
BABA YAGA 42
The Legend of the Invisible Helpers - *Russia* 44
ZARQA AL-YAMAMA 46
The Legend of the Himyarite Attack - *Arabia* 48
JEON WOO-CHI 50
The Legend of the Heavenly Messenger - *Korea* 52
SUN WUKONG 54
The Legend of the Monkey King - *China* 56
MARIE LAVEAU 58
The Legend of the Queen of Voodoo - *USA* 60
QUIZ 62

INTRODUCTION

There you are! Hello! I've been waiting for you!

My name is Aria, and before you go any further, I need to explain something very important: the book you have in your hands (yes, this one!) isn't filled with boring stuff you already know. To the contrary!

The book you're reading is a real, authentic, unique, inimitable journal written by a true expert on legendary witches and wizards. (The expert, in all modesty, is me!)

Are you curious yet?

What's that? Of course you have to believe in magic! Trust me. I really love wizards, sorceresses, magicians, and fairies. Well, to be totally honest, I grew up in a family where everyone loved magic. My parents had a giant collection of books on the topic and I've read them all. Really, truly all of them!

Don't believe it? Read this book and you'll see! In it, I've written all that I've learned and discovered about some of the most important, most magical people of all time. Some of them lived in faraway lands, while others come from nearby; some became famous and others didn't. But they all had an incredible gift for magic.

Sadly, I didn't meet them myself, because they lived a long, long, long time ago. Who knows how many other wizards, witches, and sorcerers exist today, hidden in the furthest corners of the earth, where you'd least expect them. Who knows, maybe someday you'll meet one. So, don't let this opportunity get away! Read my journal carefully, think about the stories and notes in it, and get ready for a great adventure.

That's enough chitchat for now. Turn the page and dive into the mysterious and surprising world of magic!

MORGAN LE FAY

Let's begin! I'm about to tell you about a fairy that you've probably heard of already: the ultra-famous Morgan le Fay. In some stories, she was the head of a group of sorceresses who met (who knows, maybe they still do) every night near the dilapidated castles of England. What were they up to? Something wonderful! They used their powers to bring those ruins back to their original splendor. For example, if a castle was reduced to a pile of stones covered in moss, all it took was a magic formula to rebuild it with tall, robust walls and to fill its rooms with fine furniture and precious fabrics. Too bad that Morgan and the other sorceresses didn't make their spells last forever. Before they left, they made sure that everything they had rebuilt crumbled to the ground. This, sadly, is why we've never seen the results of their magic spells.

Morgan was a powerful fairy who could turn herself and others into animals or things.

They say that Morgan was the half-sister of King Arthur, the famous royal who gathered the Knights of the Round Table.

She often created visions of castles in the air or on land to attract sailors to the horizon, then steal their treasure.

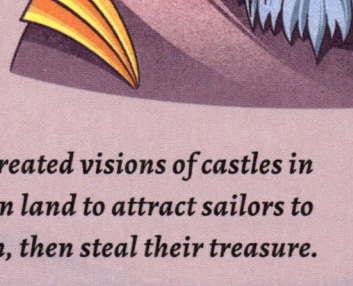

THE LEGEND OF MORGAN AND KING ARTHUR
ENGLAND

The fact that Morgan was the half-sister of King Arthur doesn't mean the two were close friends. To the contrary! It seems that the fairy did everything she could to stop the endeavors of her brother. This story is proof.

One day, Morgan decided to take one of the most precious things belonging to King Arthur: Excalibur, his magic sword. To do so, she cast a spell that created a mirage: one of her splendid castles on the surface of the ocean. When King Arthur saw the mysterious palace, he wanted to get there as fast as he could, and conveniently, Morgan offered him a ride on an enchanted ship. Once on board, the fairy made the vision disappear and, in the blink of an eye, stole his sword! She swapped it out for a copy, and he didn't notice a thing. Morgan, however, wasn't interested in keeping Excalibur for herself. She had other plans. She wanted to free herself from Arthur! So, she took the real sword to another knight named Accolon, then convinced Arthur to challenge him to a duel. Luckily, Arthur knew she was up to something and he fought really hard, until Excalibur was back in his hands.

But Morgan wasn't going to give up so easily. To keep putting spokes in the wheels of her able, powerful brother, she used a bit of magic to put Lancelot, the most famous knight of the Round Table, in prison.

Too bad for her, this plan failed, too. So, to reach her goal, she joined the knights in Arthur's service who were plotting against him, envious of his power and wanting to take over his kingdom. Thanks to the help of the sorceress, the knights surprised the king, challenging him to a battle in which they wounded him.

At that point, something happened that left everyone speechless. Morgan redeemed herself, coming to the aid of her struggling brother and taking him to Avalon to cure him with her magic, up until the day of his glorious return. After this plot twist, Morgan and Arthur finally made peace with each other.

MERLIN

Merlin was the quintessential magician, famous around the world.

He was really unique and sometimes a bit scatterbrained, but don't be fooled! In reality, he was one of the most powerful wizards of all time. But that's not all. He was also an expert in science and art (that's right, even wizards study things besides magic!). Perhaps his hobbies were what helped make his spells special and practically infallible.

Merlin lived in a big cave and he was originally from England (he's often one of the characters in stories about King Arthur), but he also appears in lots of legends from other countries.

In other words, he's world famous, like a true star!

The story goes that Merlin was the one to move the giant boulders of Stonehenge from Ireland to England.

Merlin could change his appearance, meaning he was a shape-shifter who could turn into any animal, from an owl to an ant.

In some stories, Merlin is described as a sort of practitioner of black magic, very different from the nice, jovial wizard of traditional legends.

Since he was a boy, Merlin had been able to see the future.

VIVIAN

Now that you know who Merlin is, I can tell you about the famous, powerful fairy he was in love with: Vivian.

Young and beautiful, Vivian had many great qualities, but her best one was her generosity. That's right. She had a big heart and she was always ready to help others. That's why everyone loved and respected her. At the same time, however, she was very smart and determined (maybe a little stubborn, too!). She was willing to work hard and use her magic to get what she wanted. And no one could change her mind!

Basically, Vivian was a lot like modern heroines: kind and tough!

Vivian was also called the "Lady of the Lake."

Vivian lived at the bottom of a lake, in a wonderful palace, in the Brocéliande Forest.

They say that this fairy is still alive and that she spends her days in her underwater home, only heading to the surface every so often, without ever being seen.

Vivian was the one who gave Merlin the famous sword called Excalibur, the one that Arthur pulled from the stone to become king.

THE LEGEND OF THE BROCÉLIANDE FOREST
FRANCE

A few years ago, some experts discovered a stone tomb in the Brocéliande Forest. So they conducted some studies, and they found out that it was the final resting place of the great Merlin! But why there, in that forest? Well, it has to be due to the fact that he was in love with the fairy Vivian.

One day, Vivian left her castle at the bottom of the lake and headed to the surface. Walking in the woods, she heard an unfamiliar voice. It was chanting magic spells! Curious, the fairy drew closer and saw a wizard who was casting some really extraordinary spells, turning himself into a different animal each time.

Vivian immediately realized that it was the great Merlin, so she introduced herself. The magician, for his part, instantly fell in love with the beautiful fairy and asked her to marry him. So, she proposed a pact: once the day came when Merlin had taught her all his spells, she would say yes. (I told you that Vivian was smart and determined!) The wizard agreed.

But, once she had learned all the secrets of his magic, Vivian didn't keep her end of the promise and returned to the bottom of the lake. Poor Merlin was so sad that he stayed there, in the forest, forever waiting for her.

Today, in that place, there are two rocks, forming the tomb of the betrayed, smitten wizard.

CIRCE

The time has come to talk about someone very special: the oldest sorceress in Western literature. Maybe you've heard about her at school, or even read about her in a book. Her name is Circe, the minor goddess and daughter of the sun god Helios and the Ocean nymph Perse.

This wizard is able to turn herself and anyone else into any creature: she inherited this extraordinary power from her father. But that isn't all! Her mother gave her a beautiful voice, with which Circe can enchant whoever hears her talk or sing.

That's why the name Circe is often used to indicate someone who can easily convince others to do what they want.

Circe is often represented with a golden wand or staff, in the act of casting a spell.

She appears in famous tales from classic Western mythology, such as the **Odyssey** *and epic poems about the* **Argonauts**.

She knows all the magic herbs and how to make lots of different magic potions.

THE LEGEND OF CIRCE AND ODYSSEUS
Greece

Circe lives on a remote, very wild island: her home is protected by ferocious beasts that scare anyone except Circe, with whom they act like sweet little puppies. One day, the hero Odysseus landed on Circe's island and, well, keep reading to find out!

For many years, Odysseus (who is also known as Ulysses), the brave king of Ithaca and star of the *Odyssey*, had been sailing the Mediterranean Sea with his travel companions. One day, they landed on the island of Aeaea (that's the name of Circe's island).

Odysseus asked a few sailors to explore the island, which seemed to be deserted. In the meantime, he would wait on the ship. As they walked, the men heard a melodious voice, so they followed it. Where do you think it led them? That's right! Circe's house!

She welcomed them enthusiastically, calming the beasts that protected the entry and offering them a wonderful banquet. However, instead of water, she poured a magic potion into their cups.

Then guess what happened? They all were turned into pigs!

Well, except one of them: Eurylochus. That's because he realized something was amiss, so he only pretended to drink his glass of potion. Without Circe noticing, he managed to escape and warn Odysseus of the danger ahead.

When Odysseus found out what had happened, he realized that Circe would soon have turned him and the rest of his crew into pigs, too!

Escaping to somewhere safe would have been the simplest solution, but being a true hero, he wanted to save his friends and turn them back into people.

Luckily, at that very moment, the god Hermes came to help him. By the way, Odysseus had a few gods as friends (and a few as enemies, too!): Hermes gave him a magic plant that could block all of Circe's spells.

So, Odysseus went to the sorceress and managed to convince her to turn all of his sailors back into men. At that point, Circe was so fascinated by his courage that she asked him to stay on the island with his crew, at least until they were ready to depart again. That's right! She fell in love with him!

But she had a plan: she wanted to enchant him with her voice, so that he would stay with her forever. Luckily, Odysseus had the magic plant Hermes had given him: he deflected Circe's spell and set sail to Ithaca.

MELINDA

You think all witches are bad? Well, you're mistaken, and the woman I'm about to tell you about will prove it. Melinda, an Italian witch with a lovely name, spent her days casting good, kind magic spells. Every so often, she would cast a mean one, but only when someone had done something really bad.

Sadly, no one ever really understood that Melinda had such a big heart. In fact, the poor witch never had any friends and she lived her entire life in the mountains of Abruzzo, Italy, in a shack with a dirt floor and a wood roof. Putting it lightly, her house wasn't exactly beautiful, in part because she spent all her time on magic and she didn't often clean.

To cast her spells, Melinda used very simple ingredients: a stew of poisonous mushrooms, buttons, wild herbs, and old rags.

She had eyes as thin as pins, a pointy nose, and a protruding lower lip. Seen from the side, her profile resembled that of Dante Alighieri.

Melinda was the mother of twins, both of them were boys.

Despite being a little old lady, her hair hadn't changed since she was a child: as black and shiny as a raven's feather.

THE LEGEND OF MELINDA
ITALY

I'm sure that now you want to know all there is to know about Melinda. And I'm ready to tell you her exciting story! I have to warn you that it's a little sad, though the ending will surprise you.

Melinda cast her first spell when she was still very young. Can you guess what it was for? To make the boy she liked fall in love with her: it seems that he wasn't very interested in her at first. Her first foray into witchcraft was the preparation of a love potion, like the ones you hear about in fairy tales. She used very simple ingredients: a lock of her hair, a button, and a piece of fabric. Her beloved drank it and…POOF! He immediately fell in love with her and they got married. After a few months, they had twins, but their happiness didn't last. Melinda's husband soon had to leave to fight in the war, and he never came home (I told you it was a sad story). The poor witch found herself facing hardships and, having two little boys to take care of, she decided to turn what she did best—magic—into a job. So, she went to take classes from two wizards, one specialized in good spells, the other in evil ones.

After studying really hard, Melinda, who was a witch by birth but also out of need, dedicated her life to the craft. As payment for the good spells she cast, she made do with the things her clients gave her in exchange: a few coins, a head of garlic, a sack of potatoes, and the like. For evil spells, on the other hand, Melinda asked for much, much more because she didn't like doing them. Unfortunately, the people of the town avoided her because they didn't understand that she actually was a very kind person. Even her sons abandoned her as soon as they could, moving far, far away. Melinda was left all alone with her spells, for the rest of her life. She knew very well that, when her time came, the devil would come to take her soul, just as had happened to other witches who dealt in nefarious arts. But, unlike the others, she was one step ahead of him. How? Well, she had a carpenter make a big hole in the roof of her house, so that her soul could escape at the right moment, finally flying free in the sky above the mountains of Abruzzo.

TÁLTOS

The next sorcerer has a special name, suitable for a wizard with special powers. Or maybe a shaman is a more accurate term. The táltos is a very, very important figure in the traditions of Hungarian populations. In reality, there is more than one táltos: there are lots of them and they can be male or female. It's important to remember that detail, so it's easier to recognize them, if you ever run into one!

These shamans have a special, noble mission: they must always take care of their community. OK, but what does that mean exactly? They help community members when they're sick, but also when they're sad or worried, thanks to their incredible magic powers. All the táltos has to do is stop and think, maybe meditate a bit, to find the best solution to every problem. Then they immediately put it into practice… with magic!

The táltos is often born with an extra finger or two, or born with a full set of teeth.

The moments in which they stop to meditate and think are called "révülés."

These shamans can cure any illness or fight any evil. Another important mission of theirs is to protect the community from enemies.

THE LEGEND OF THE SEVENTH YEAR
HUNGARY

Now that you know what a táltos is, I want to reveal a secret about them: unfortunately, these shamans aren't entirely invincible or immortal. Find out why in the short story below.

The most important year (I mean really, really important) in the life of a táltos isn't the first and it isn't the tenth either. It's the seventh! Why? Well, the reason is hard to guess. Up until they turn seven years old, their enemies can take a tooth from these shamans, which deprives them of all of their special magic powers. Sometimes it's their parents who pull out one of their teeth; that way no one steals their táltos child. Sure, it's a hard decision to make, because the táltos won't ever then be able to help their community as they were meant to. Luckily, before they turn seven, táltos children are often sent to stay with older táltos for three full nights (a short, yet very intense time!) so that they can teach them about the magical powers they possess. That way, the children learn how to defend themselves and to protect their precious teeth up to their fateful birthday.

THE WITCH OF GIRONA

Let me introduce you to another witch, this time from Spain.

The witch of Girona, a city in the northeast of the country, was unlike other sorceresses: she would only cast "evil" spells. That's right. Her spells were always negative and used to spite people or put someone in a predicament.

Sure, this witch wasn't beloved by the people of the city, but she didn't care one bit. For her entire life, she was cantankerous, crabby, and spiteful, making the people mad in any way possible. She liked being that way, and unfortunately, no one managed to make her change. Too bad!

She specialized in curses: all she had to do was say one of her magic formulas and it was done.

The witch of Girona had a strange, dangerous habit of throwing rocks against the walls of the city's cathedral.

The people of Girona would often lock themselves indoors so they wouldn't run into her.

THE LEGEND OF THE CATHEDRAL OF GIRONA
SPAIN

As I said, the witch of Girona had the very bad habit of throwing rocks at the city's main church. Until she had to give up this pastime once and for all.

One evening, the witch of Girona came to the city's cathedral, and as always, she picked up a few stones and rocks, throwing them at the walls of the building. It was her favorite pastime!

SMASH! BANG! CLANG! All that racket drew a few locals to their windows. They knew her well by then, but they still complained and tried asking her to stop (never say never!). But the witch didn't listen and she kept going, throwing the stones even harder as a satisfied sneer crept across her face.

That continued until she was hit by a very bright light and she was magically turned into a stone statue!

The people were shocked and went to the square to see it. Was it the witch herself who cast that spell gone wrong? Anyway, they realized that someone invisible (nobody knows who) had transformed her forever.

So they placed her on the wall of the church, turning her into a gargoyle, which is a sort of rain gutter.

No more spells were uttered from that mouth. From that day on, only rainwater came from it!

UNDINES

The sorceresses that I'm going to tell you about are very similar to mermaids: "undines." I love their name and I feel like it's quite accurate, given that these creatures often live near rivers, springs, ponds, waterfalls, or lakes. Near water, basically!

They say that undines don't have a soul but that they can get one by marrying a mortal. For that very reason, they spend their days swimming near the surface of the water in search of the right person for them.

Their beautiful singing is their magic power, which they use to bewitch sailors.

In general, these creatures are good and kind, despite having a bit of a temper. If someone tricks them or offends them in some way, they get revenge through magic! Yeah, it's best not to mess with undines.

Their favorite pastimes are singing, dancing in the waves, and weaving seaweed.

The sound of their voice resembles flowing water and is very musical and relaxing.

Undines are beautiful creatures who often have a tail like a fish, just like the Little Mermaid.

THE LEGEND OF LORELEI
Germany

This is the story of a special undine, one who lived in the water of the River Rhine, in Germany. Her way of doing things put her in danger.

Lorelei was a beautiful undine with a very dangerous habit: she distracted sailors with her magical singing, causing them to be shipwrecked.

One day, a rich man ordered his soldiers to capture Lorelei, seeking revenge for the son he lost in one of those shipwrecks. Unfortunately, he didn't consider the fact that the song of the undine could hypnotize everyone: even his soldiers were at risk of crashing their ship! But the noble man wanted to capture her at all costs, so he sent his soldiers out on a mission once again, this time wearing wax ear plugs.

Immune to her magic song, the men were about to capture her, but her father appeared

and saved her! How? He created a giant foam horse and he sent it galloping towards the soldiers, who escaped, scared out of their wits. Lorelei then managed to hide in the depths of the river. But she never came back.

The rock that it's said she used to appear on is still named after her today.

BABA YAGA

Have you ever heard of Baba Yaga? Perhaps! This witch is famous even today and her look is entirely unique. She is often portrayed flying in the sky, up high in the clouds. Yet one of the characteristics for which she's most often remembered is...her house! Baba Yaga lives in a hut built on two giant chicken legs, while the gate to her garden is made of bones and decorated by skulls. And the lock? Well, it's shaped like a mouth full of pointed teeth! Basically, her house is as scary as she is! You should also know that this witch ages a year every time she's asked a question. She can get a bit younger in only one way: drinking a special tea made from blue roses. That's why she lets anyone who gives them to her make a wish to thank them for their help. And that's the only time when Baba Yaga is nice to those who ask her to do something!

To fly, Baba Yaga sits astride a kitchen mortar and uses the pestle as a rudder.

The two chicken legs, which are the base for her hut, run and jump about, taking her wherever she wants to go!

Baba Yaga often gets mad because she gets too many questions (which make her age a lot!).

She has fun erasing trails in the woods, using a broom made of silver birch branches.

THE LEGEND OF THE INVISIBLE HELPERS
RUSSIA

Baba Yaga is the protagonist of many tales, scary and otherwise. I like the one I'm about to tell you quite a lot because it has to do with a brave girl with a big heart.

Vasilisa lived with her father in a modest house. One day, the fire in their hearth went out. They tried to light it again, but they realized it was impossible. Vasilisa's father told her that it had to be a magic spell. Only Baba Yaga could help them get the fire going again. So, Vasilisa went out into the woods to visit the witch. After having walked for a very long time, she finally reached the famous house with the chicken legs (so scary!). The witch welcomed her, but as soon as Vasilisa asked about the fire, she got annoyed and locked the girl in a cage made of bones (just like her gate). She promised to free the girl if she cleaned the entire house, which was a true mess, by that evening! Vasilisa accepted, even if the mission seemed impossible. Luckily, while she was working hard, she met some magic helpers who had broken into the house: they were ready to help her! They were a cat, a small tree that could walk, and a dog. They all could make themselves invisible so that the witch couldn't see them. Thanks to their help and her hard work, Vasilisa completed the task in time. Baba Yaga, impressed, let her go home, where her father was waiting with open arms.

ZARQA AL-YAMAMA

Have you ever heard of Zarqa Al-Yamama? I bet you haven't. Don't worry. I'll tell you everything about her. Zarqa was an incredibly talented and respected Arabian sorceress who was gifted with incredible magic powers. In fact, she could see the future. No, she didn't use a crystal ball like fortune tellers do. She could see things that were about to happen thanks to her incredible blue eyes, which shone as bright as diamonds every time she used her magic. For this very reason, she is often portrayed with large, deep, shimmering eyes.

Zarqa was part of the legendary ancient Tasm population, which lived next to the Jadīs people, the tribe that her husband belonged to.

She was a beautiful, cultured woman who cared deeply about the appearance of her precious blue eyes. She was the first woman to line her eyes with kohl, the soft black pencil that is still used as eyeliner today.

In Arabic, her name means "the blue-eyed woman from Yamama."

She would use antimony powder, a chemical substance, as an eyewash to care for her extraordinary sight.

THE LEGEND OF THE HIMYARITE ATTACK
Arabia

Like I was saying, Zarqa was respected by her people and everyone counted on her. But on one occasion, her people didn't believe her, and they paid for it dearly. Keep reading to find out what happened.

One day, a tubba (a sort of Yemeni king) named Hassān Abū Karib invaded Yamama, the land of the Tasm people, with his men, the Himyarites. As always, Zarqa's blue eyes let her see the army coming from far away, a full three days in advance! She ran to warn her people, sure that they would be able to organize a counter-attack and chase the invaders away. However, the enemy soldiers en route knew all about Zarqa (though not as well as they thought).

So, to avoid being defeated, they devised a plan: they gathered a few tree branches and brought them with them to hide behind. However, Zarqa's gift was so powerful that she noticed their trap. She warned her tribe that the trees were moving towards them and, most importantly, that soldiers were hidden behind them. To her dismay, the members of her tribe didn't believe her and chose to ignore her warning. It turned out that Zarqa was right, and in the end the enemy soldiers arrived and beat the Tasm, taking the powerful blue-eyes sorceress prisoner.

JEON WOO-CHI

Jeon Woo-chi was a Korean scholar capable of completing incredible magical feats. He lived during the Joseon dynasty and many see him as the most important "sorcerer" in Korean history. He appears in many ancient books under the name Woosa, which means "featherman" (don't ask me why, I still don't know!).

He began studying magic when he was very young, and to avoid all distraction, he took refuge in an isolated temple in the mountains (he was really determined!). They say that his powers were so incredible that he could even heal the sick and end the most serious epidemics. Surely, his intention was to do good and help those in need, which is why he became so famous.

He had many students who were by his side to learn his magic, but none of them ever reached his level.

He's so famous that movies and TV shows have been made about his adventures.

According to legend, Woo-chi got some of his powers from a fox who had taken on the appearance of a woman to trick him.

50

He had a kind, nice face. Some say that he wore glasses.

THE LEGEND OF THE HEAVENLY MESSENGER
KOREA

When a terrible famine struck Korea, Jeon Woo-chi decided to use his extraordinary powers to help the needy, but not everyone appreciated his generosity. Let me tell you why.

To put his plan into action, Jeon Woo-chi went to the king. Thanks to his magical powers, he convinced the king he was a heavenly messenger and that he needed a lot of gold to build a new castle in the sky. The king, of course, fell for it and gave Jeon the gold he asked for. Once he had what he wanted, however, the sorcerer didn't use the riches to build something or even for personal gain. He gave the gold to the poor people of the city, who celebrated him like a true hero! But the king soon found out, and angered at having been tricked, he ordered his army to capture Jeon. Luckily, the royal guards failed in their mission, as Jeon used his magical powers to flee. But then he regretted it; he didn't want to disobey the orders of the king. So, he went back to the royal palace to ask for forgiveness. Enthralled once again by his powers, the king forgave him and even asked him to come work at the royal palace. But Jeon was a free spirit, so he kindly refused and disappeared once again, never to be seen.

SUN WUKONG

Did you know there's a very important figure in both Chinese and Japanese cultures? He's so famous that he often appears in stories under different names. But no matter, he's easy to recognize by his unmistakable features. Who am I talking about? Oops! I forgot to tell you his name: Sun Wukong. It's a very musical name, isn't it? Easier to remember that way.

Sun Wukong is a very special magician, with a very special appearance: despite being a man, he looks a lot like a monkey! Actually, lots of people know him as the Monkey King (he has that exact role in the legend I'm about to tell you).

OK, I've explained almost everything. There's just one more interesting detail you should know…

Sun Wukong is impulsive, lively, and always ready for a fight: his weapon is an extensible rod.

He has a group of close, trusted friends. They go on adventures together and often have to confront lots of enemies.

Sun Wukong wears a small crown on his head, making him look like a real king.

THE LEGEND OF THE MONKEY KING
CHINA

The main character of the story I'm about to tell you is none other than Sun Wukong. In this tale, he proves to have great courage and to be committed to his people. Find out why.

Since the beginning, the monkey population struggled to find enough food, and Sun Wukong, who saw what was happening, decided to help them. So he brought some flowers and some fruit to a cave, a safe space he had himself discovered, where food was boundless.

To thank him, the monkeys decided he would be their king, which made Sun very happy. However, he worried that an unexpected event would cause him to lose this prestigious role. So he decided to consult an old wise man, the patriarch Subhūti. To do so, he had to set out on a long journey to reach him, but it was worth it! That's because Subhūti would teach him how to be immortal! This made him a truly powerful warrior, able to transform into 72 different animals and people and to fly on a cloud. In the end, Sun returned to the cave and taught the monkeys and other animals how to fight, conquering and subjugating all the other species.

Sun Wukong, however, still wasn't happy: he wanted more! So he went to see the Dragon Kings of the Four Seas, and he asked each of them for a gift to become invincible: a staff that extended and retracted as he needed, a phoenix-feather cap, golden chain mail, and a pair of magic boots. With these weapons and immortality, the sorcerer still rules the monkey population, which respects and admires him.

MARIE LAVEAU

In New Orleans, Louisiana, there once lived a woman named Marie Laveau, a famous witch who was respected and a bit feared by all. She prepared all types of potions and jealously guarded her secrets. What ingredients did she use? Just a warning: they're sort of gross, but by now it's too late to change your mind! Laveau used herbs, oils, stones, bones, hair, fingernail clippings, and even filth. She was a powerful practitioner of Voodoo: they say she could cast spells and curses so effective that they impacted the people they were directed at and all their family members. Even the ones that weren't born yet! Undoubtedly, it was better to stay on her good side.

Laveau wasn't just a witch: she also had a hair salon, which was frequented by the wealthiest ladies of the city.

Her unusual choice of pet was famous in all of New Orleans. Can you guess what it was? A giant snake named Zombie!

In addition to being known for her curses, Laveau was also known for her willingness to help anyone who needed a hand.

She often wore a colorful, bold tignon head wrap and an orange shawl that extended down to her knees.

THE LEGEND OF THE QUEEN OF VOODOO
UNITED STATES OF AMERICA

Marie Laveau practiced the magic known as Voodoo, which often involves casting spells with small dolls that resemble the people they represent. She was so good at it that everyone asked her for help. Of course, to get that good, she had to study really hard.

Laveau was lucky to be born a free woman at a time when, in New Orleans, lots of people of African origin (like her) were enslaved. Her mother was enslaved until she married Marie's father, a rich businessman who lived in the city. Thanks to him, the example he set, and his encouragement, his daughter learned to read and write at a young age. She quickly learned about all types of herbs and flowers and, studying and practicing a lot, she learned various rituals to purify people's souls of their sins, but also to punish people who behaved poorly. Despite being so young, she soon became very famous. Her magic spells were always the most effective and everyone considered her a true Voodoo sorceress.

So, lots of people began to ask her for help. For example, some people would ask her to make a potion that would solve all the problems of their love life, others wanted good luck, and others needed healing balms. In terms of her negative spells, on the other hand, she often needed to use a few spells to scare people who had done bad things or to take back something they had stolen, so that they would regret it. Laveau never said no to anyone and she practiced her magic for her entire life, helping those in need.

QUIZ

Perhaps you haven't read the entire book up to this page. Or maybe you have. In any case, I have a surprise for you! I created a sort of final game, so you can see how much you've learned from reading my journal. Let's begin!

1 How many children did **Melinda** have?

A - None
B - Two
C - Three

2 What does the nickname Woosa mean, given to **Jeon Woo-Chi**?

A - "Featherman"
B - "Magicman"
C - "Man of 1,000 powers"

3 Who was the half-brother of **Morgan Le Fay**?

A - Lancelot
B - Merlin
C - King Arthur

4 What did **Sun Wukong** fly on?

A - A cloud
B - A rainbow
C - The sun

5 What American city did **Marie Laveau** live in?

A - New York
B - New Orleans
C - Los Angeles

6 Which flower helped **Baba Yaga** become younger?

A - A red tulip
B - A yellow daisy
C - A blue rose

7 Are the **Táltos** men or women?

A - They can be men or women
B - Men
C - Women

8 What was the name of the island that **Circe** lived on?

A - Aeia
B - Aeaea
C - Eaua

9 What fairy did **Merlin** fall in love with?

A - Morgan
B - Melinda
C - Vivian

10 What was **Lorelei's** special power?

A - Her magical voice
B - Creating waves
C - Making potions

IF YOU GOT ONLY 5 POINTS (OR LESS):

No problem!
All you need to do is re-read a few pages of this journal. That's not so bad!

Take your time reviewing the stories and notes you don't remember and then try again. We're all here to learn and become experts!

IF YOU SCORED AT LEAST 6 POINTS:

Congratulations! Great job!
Magicians, witches, táltos, shamans, and undines have no more secrets for you.

Keep going and never stop seeking out magic creatures.
I'll keep doing the same!

ANSWERS

1-B; 2-A; 3-C; 4-A; 5-B; 6-C; 7-A; 8-B; 9-C; 10-A

Anna Láng

Anna Láng is a Hungarian graphic designer and illustrator currently living and working in Milan. After attending the Hungarian University of Fine Arts in Budapest and graduating as a graphic designer in 2011, she worked for three years at an advertising agency. She was awarded the Békéscsaba City Prize at the Hungarian Biennial of Graphic Design with the Shakespeare Poster Series in 2013. She currently works in the genre she is most passionate about: illustrations for children's books. She has created the illustrations for various books for White Star Kids in recent years.

Tea Orsi

Even as a child, Tea Orsi loved making up stories, writing them down and even illustrating them with small, brightly colored drawings. As the years passed, her passion for writing didn't fade. Today, Orsi writes scripts for animated series and is the author of comics, books, and magazines for children. Her days are spent in the company of princesses, fairies, and other fantastical characters, always ready for fun new adventures on television or in print. She lives in Parma, Italy, with her family and two cute little dogs and loves to travel the world, looking for ideas and details that can inspire new stories yet to be told.

WS whitestar kids™ is a trademark of White Star s.r.l.

© 2024 White Star s.r.l.
Piazzale Luigi Cadorna, 6 - 20123 Milan, Italy
www.whitestar.it

Translation: Katherine Kirby
Editing: Abby Young

All rights reserved. No part of this publication may be reproduced, stored or transmitted in any form or by any means without written permission from the publisher.

First printing, July 2024

ISBN 978-88-544-2090-8
1 2 3 4 5 6   28 27 26 25 24

Printed and manufactured in China by
Shenzhen Dream Colour Printing Company Limited,
Shenzhen, Guangdong